Miss Bea's Seas

Louisa Harding

ROWAN

Are you having fun Miss Bea,
running in and out of the waves?

Wave Jacket instructions page 28

Ciaran finds a good stone to throw
way out into the sea.

Look out Oscar,
a crab might nibble your toes!

Target Slipover instructions page 32

Miss Bea uses a bucket and spade
to dig a great big hole.

Ciaran lifts his yellow bucket,
"come and look at my sandcastle".

Have you caught a fish Oscar?
"No, only shells and stones".

Emma sits in a little blue boat
and eats her jam sandwiches.

There are more boats in the harbour.
Miss Bea feeds the birds with her left-over lunch.

Walking along the water's edge,
Miss Bea hears the Ice cream van.

Livvy licks a lovely ice-cream
a perfect end to a perfect seaside day.

Sail Jacket instructions page 46

The Knitting Patterns
Information Page

Introduction
The knitwear in 'Miss Bea's Seaside' has been designed using Rowan Denim yarn, this is an Idigo dyed yarn with very unique properties. The yarn is very hard-wearing and machine washable, On page 27 you will find more information regarding this yarn's special characteristics.

The knitting patterns
Each pattern has a chart and simple written instructions that have been colour coded making the different sizes easier to identify. E.g. if you are knitting age 2–3 years follow the instructions in red where you are given a choice. The patterns are laid out as follows:

Age/Size Diagrams
The ages given and the corresponding diagrams are a guide only. The measurements for each knitted piece are shown in a size diagram at the start of every pattern. As all children vary, make sure you choose the right garment size, do this by measuring an item of your child's clothing you like the fit of. Choose the instruction size accordingly. If still unsure, knit a larger size, as children always grow.

Yarn
This indicates the amount of yarn needed to complete the design. All the garments that use more than one shade of yarn will have the amount used for each shade.

Needles
Listed are the suggested knitting needles used to make the garment. The smaller needles are usually used for edgings or ribs, the larger needles for the main body fabric.

Buttons/Zips
This indicates the number of buttons or length of zip needed to fasten the finished garment.

Tension
Tension is the single most important factor when you begin knitting. The fabric tension is written for example as 20 sts x 28 rows to 10cm measured over stocking stitch using 4 mm (US 6) needles before washing. Each pattern is worked out mathematically, if the correct tension is not achieved the garment pieces will not measure the size stated in the diagram.

Before embarking on knitting your garment we recommend you check your tension as follows: Using the needle size given cast on 5–10 more stitches than stated in the tension, and work 5–10 more rows. When you have knitted your tension square lay it on a flat surface, place a rule or tape measure horizontally, count the number of stitches equal to the distance of 10cm. Place the measure vertically and count the number of rows, these should equal the tension given in the pattern. If you have too many stitches to 10cm, try again using a thicker needle, if you have too few stitches to 10cm use a finer needle.
Note: Check your tension regularly as you knit - once you become relaxed and confident with your knitting, your tension can change.
Please refer to page 27 regarding washing and making up instructions for Rowan Denim yarn.

Back
This is the start of your pattern. Following the colour code for your chosen size, you will be instructed how many stitches to cast on and to work from chart and written instructions as follows:

Knitting from charts
Each square on a chart represents one stitch; each line of squares indicates a row of knitting. When working from the chart, read odd numbered rows (right side of fabric) from right to left and even numbered rows (wrong side of fabric) from left to right.
Each separate colour used is given a letter and on some charts a corresponding symbol. The different stitches used are also represented by a symbol, e.g. knit and purl, a key to each symbol is with each chart.

Front (Fronts) and Sleeves
The pattern continues with instructions to make these garment pieces.

Pressing
Once you have finished knitting and washed all the pieces it is important that all the pieces are pressed, see page 48 for more details.

Neckband (front bands)
This instruction tells you how to work any finishing off

needed to complete your garment, such as knitting a neckband on a sweater or edgings on a cardigan. Once you have completed all the knitting you can begin to make up your garment, see page 48 for making up instructions.

Abbreviations
In the pattern you will find some of the most common words used have been abbreviated:

K	knit
P	purl
st(s)	stitches
inc	increase(e)(ing) knit into the front and back of next st to make 2 stitches.
dec	decreas(e)(ing)
st st	stocking stitch (right side row knit, wrong side row purl)
garter st	garter stitch (knit every row)
beg	begin(ning)
foll	follow(ing)
rem	remain(ing)
rev	reverse(ing)
rep	repeat
alt	alternate
cont	continue
patt	pattern
tog	together
cm	centimetres
in(s)	inch(es)
RS	right side
WS	wrong side
K2tog	knit two sts together to make one stitch
tbl	through back of loop
yo	yarn over, bring yarn over needle before working next st to create an extra loop.
M1P	make one stitch by picking up horizontal loop before next stitch and purling into back of it.
CN	cable needle
C4B	slip next 2 sts onto CN, hold at back, K2, K2 from CN.
C4F	slip next 2 sts onto CN, hold at front, K2, K2 from CN.
C8B	slip next 4 sts onto CN, hold at back, K4, K4 from CN.

Knitting Techniques
A simple learn to knit guide

Introduction

Using illustrations and simple written instructions we have put together a beginners guide to knitting. With a basic knowledge of the simplest stitches you can create your own unique handknitted garments.

When you begin to knit you feel very clumsy, all fingers and thumbs. This stage passes as confidence and experience grows. Many people are put off hand knitting thinking that they are not using the correct techniques of holding needles, yarn or working of stitches, all knitters develop their own style, so please persevere.

Casting On

This is the term used for making a row of stitches; the foundation row for each piece of knitting. Make a slip knot. Slip this onto a needle. This is the basis of the two casting on techniques as shown below.

Thumb Cast On

This method uses only one needle and gives a neat, but elastic edge. Make a slip knot 1 metre from the cut end of the yarn, you use this length to cast on the stitches. For a knitted piece, the length between cut end and slip knot can be difficult to judge, allow approx 3 times the width measurement.

     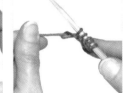

1. Make a slip knot approx 1 metre from the end of the yarn, with ball of yarn to your right.	2. Hold needle in RH. With the cut end of yarn held in LH, wrap yarn around your thumb from left to right anti-clockwise to front.	3. Insert RH needle into yarn around thumb, take yarn attached to ball around the back of RH needle to front.	4. Draw through needle to make a loop.	5. Pull on both ends of yarn gently. Creating a stitch on right hand needle.	6. Repeat from 2. until the required number of stitches has been cast on.

Cable Cast On

This method uses two needles; it gives a firm neat finish. It is important that you achieve an even cast on, this may require practice.

1. With slip knot on LH needle, insert RH needle. Take yarn behind RH needle; bring yarn forward between needles.	2. Draw the RH needle back through the slip knot, making a loop on RH needle with yarn.	3. Slip this loop onto left hand needle; taking care not to pull the loop too tight.	4. Insert the RH needle between the two loops on LH needle. Take yarn behind RH needle; bring forward, between needles.	5. Draw through the RH needle making a loop as before. Slip this stitch onto LH needle.	6. Repeat from 4. until the required number of stitches has been cast on.

How to Knit -
The knit stitch is the simplest to learn. By knitting every row you create garter stitch and the simplest of all knitted fabrics.

1. Hold the needle with the cast-on stitches in LH. Insert RH needle into first stitch.

2. Take yarn around the back of RH needle, bring yarn forward between needles.

3. Draw the RH needle through the stitch. Drop loop on LH needle

4. Making a loop on RH needle with yarn. One stitch made.

5. Repeat to the end of the row.

How to Purl -
The purl stitch is a little more complicated to master. Using a combination of knit and purl stitches together forms the bases of most knitted fabrics. The most common fabric knitted is stocking stitch, this is created when you knit 1 row, then purl 1 row.

  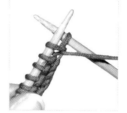  

1. Hold the needle with stitches on in LH and with yarn at the front of work, insert RH needle into front of stitch.

2. Take yarn around the back of RH needle, bring yarn to front.

3. Draw the needle through from front to back, making a loop on RH needle.

4. Slip the stitch onto right hand needle. Drop loop on LH needle.

5. Repeat to the end of the row.

Joining in a new yarn -
A new ball of yarn can be joined in on either a right side or a wrong side row, but to give a neat finish it is important you do this at the start of a row. Simply drop the old yarn, start knitting with the new ball, then after a few stitches tie the two ends together in a temporary knot. These ends are then sewn into the knitting at the making up stage, see page 48.

Casting Off -
This is the method of securing stitches at the top of your knitted fabric. It is important that the cast off edge should be elastic like the rest of the fabric; if you find that your cast off is too tight, try using a larger needle. You can cast off knitwise (as illustrated), purlwise, or in a combination of stitches, such as rib.

1. Hold the needle with the stitches on in LH, knit the first stitch.

2. Knit the next stitch from LH needle, two stitches on RH needle.

3. Using the point of LH needle; insert into first stitch on RH needle.

4. Take the first stitch over the second stitch.

5. One stitch on right hand needle.

6. Rep from 2 until one stitch on RH needle. Cut yarn, draw cut end through last stitch to secure.

Knitting with Rowan Denim
Rowan Denim has been one of the most popular yarns for many years.

An attractive yarn that is also hard wearing and practical, a garment knitted in Rowan Denim is machine washable making it ideal for Children's garments.

Rope Sweater
Knitted using Rowan Denim Ecru. This garment shows the emphasis that is achieved over the cable pattern when using Rowan Denim

Sand castle Sweater
Knitted using Rowan Denim Tennessee. The detail of the simple textured stitch in this design is enhanced by the unique properties of this yarn.

Seashore Sweater
Knitted using Ecru Rowan Denim as the background with highlights of Nashville and Memphis. The garment shows that this yarn can also be used successfully in intarsia knitting.

About Rowan Denim
Rowan Denim, as with other indigo dyed textiles, fades and ages with washing and wearing. During the unconventional dying process, only the surface of the yarn is dyed, leaving the core white. Most of the colour loss takes place during the first wash when all the loose dye is washed out exposing the core. The knitted pieces will also shrink in length during the first wash. This tightens up the knitting, adding emphasis to cables and texture giving the finished garment its unique look. Rowan Denim is available in four shades, Nashville, Memphis, Tennessee and Ecru. The Ecru, which is undyed, will not change colour but like the other shades will shrink during the first wash. Some of the designs in this book use more than one colour of Rowan Denim in the same garment; some bleeding of dark shades will occur into the ecru, this is as the designer intended.

Knitting with Rowan Denim
As with all knitting patterns it is essential to achieve the tension given at the beginning of each pattern, i.e. proper shrinkage will not take place if the garment is knitted too loosely in the first place. The patterns in this book have been calculated using only Rowan Denim yarn and responsibility will not be accepted if the specified yarn has not been used. All edgings have been calculated to allow for correct shrinkage and should not be adjusted. Because the dye is only a surface dye, during knitting the colour will come off onto your hands. This will wash off very easily but it is advisable to protect your clothing or wear something dark.

Finishing off your garment
When you have completed knitting all the garment pieces you should make up the garment as follows: Sew the shoulder seams together and complete the neckband or collar and buttonbands where appropriate. The next stage is to wash all the pieces in the washing machine at a temperature of 60 - 70°C so that the shrinkage can take place. The pieces are then dried and can be sewn together. It is not essential but we do suggest that you wind some of the yarn into a small hank and wash this along with the pieces for sewing up. Once the garment is completed it can be machine washed along with similar colours.

Wave Jacket

Age 1-2 years 2-3 years 3-4 years

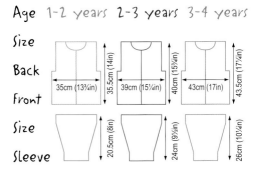

Size — Back — Front

35cm (13¾in) 39cm (15¼in) 43cm (17in)
35.5cm (14in) 40cm (15¾in) 43.5cm (17¼in)

Size — Sleeve

20.5cm (8in) 24cm (9½in) 26cm (10¼in)

Yarn

Rowan Denim x 50g balls

A. Memphis	6	7	7
B. Tennessee	3	3	3

Needles

1 pair 3 ¼ mm (US 3) needles for edging
1 pair 4 mm (US 6) needles for main body

Zip

Open-ended zip to fit

Tension

20 sts and 28 rows to 10cm measured over stocking stitch using 4mm (US 6) needles before washing

Back

Using 3 ¼ mm (US 3) needles and yarn B cast on 70,78,86 sts and work from chart A and written instructions as folls:
Chart row 1: K4,2,0 (P2, K4) 11,12,14 times, P0,2,2, K0,2,0.
Chart row 2: P4,2,0 (K2, P4) 11,12,14 times, K0,2,2, P0,2,0.

Cont in rib until chart row 20 completed.
Change to 4 mm (US 6) needles and yarn A, joining in and breaking off colours for stripe pattern as indicated on chart work in st st until row 70,80,90 completed.
Shape armhole
Cast off 6 sts at the beg next 2 rows. (58,66,74 sts)
Now working from chart B, join in yarn B and work in striped st st until chart row 42,46,48 completed.
Shape shoulders and back neck
Chart row 43,47,49: Knit 18,21,24 sts, turn and leave rem sts on a holder.
Chart row 44,48,50: Cast off 3 sts, purl to end.
Slip rem 15,18,21 sts onto a holder.
Rejoin yarn to rem sts, cast off centre 22,24,26 sts, knit to end. (18,21,24 sts)
Purl 1 row.
Chart row 45,49,51: Cast off 3 sts, knit to end.
Slip rem 15,18,21 sts onto a holder.

Left Front

Using 3 ¼ mm (US 3) needles and yarn B cast on 35,39,43 sts and work from chart A and written instructions as folls:
Note: 3 sts at centre front are knitted in garter st throughout and are **not** shown on chart.
Chart row 1: K4,2,0 (P2, K4) 4,5,6 times, P2, K5.
Chart row 2: K3, P2, K2, (P4, K2) 4,5,6 times, P4,2,0.
Cont until chart row 20 completed.
Change to 4 mm (US 6) needles and yarn A, joining in and breaking off colours for stripe pattern as indicated on chart work in st st until row 70,80,90 completed.
Shape armhole
Cast off 6 sts at the beg next row. (29,33,37 sts)
Purl 1 row.
Now working from chart B, join in yarn B and work in striped st st until chart row 31,35,37 completed.
Shape front neck
Chart row 32,36,38: K3, P3,4,5 sts and leave these on a holder, purl to end. (23,26,29 sts)
Knit 1 row.
Chart row 34,38,40: Cast off 4 sts at the beg next row, purl to end.
Dec 1 st at neck edge on next 4 rows. (15,18,21 sts)
Work without further shaping until chart row 44,48,50 completed.
Slip rem sts onto a holder.

Right Front

Using 3 ¼ mm (US 3) needles and yarn B cast on 35,39,43 sts and follow written instructions as follows:
Note: 3 sts at centre front are knitted in garter st

throughout and are **not** shown on chart.
Chart row 1: K5, P2, (K4, P2) 4,5,6 times, K4,2,0.
Chart row 2: P4,2,0, (K2, P4) 4,5,6 times, K2, P2, K3
Cont until chart row 20 completed.
Change to 4 mm (US 6) needles and yarn A, joining in and breaking off colours for stripe pattern as indicated on chart work in st st.
Complete to match left front, foll chart for right front and reversing shaping.

Sleeves (both alike)

Using 3 ¼ mm (US 3) needles and yarn B cast on 36,38,40 sts and work from chart A and written instructions as folls:
Chart row 1: K0,0,1, P1,2,2, (K4, P2) 5 times, K4, P1,2,2, K0,0,1.
Chart row 2: P0,0,1, K1,2,2, (P4, K2) 5 times, P4, K1,2,2, P0,0,1.
Cont until chart row 20 completed.
Change to 4 mm (US 6) needles and yarn A, joining in and breaking off colours for stripe pattern as indicate on chart work in st st..
Chart row 21: Inc into first st, knit to last st, inc into last st. (38,40,42 sts)
Chart row 22: Purl.
Cont from chart, shaping sides by inc as indicated to 56,60,64 sts.
Work without further shaping until chart row 70,80,88 completed.
Cast off.

Neckband

Join both shoulder seams by knitting sts together on the RS of garment using yarn A, as shown in techniques guide, page 48.
With RS facing and using 3 ¼ mm (US 3) needles and yarn A, patt across 6,7,8 sts on holder at right front neck, pick up and knit 12,13,14 sts up right front neck shaping, 28,30,32 sts across back neck, 12,13,14 sts down left front neck, work in patt across 6,7,8 sts on holder. (64,70,76 sts)
Rib row 1(WS): K3, (P4, K2) 9,10,11 times, P4, K3.
Rib row 2(RS): K3, (K4, P2,) 9,10,11 times, K7.
Work these 2 rows 5 times more.
Change to yarn B, work 4 more rows in rib as set.
Using yarn B cast off in rib.

Sew in all ends and wash pieces as described on page 27.
Complete jacket as shown in making up instructions, page 48. Sew in zip to top of rib at hem, leave rib at hem open.

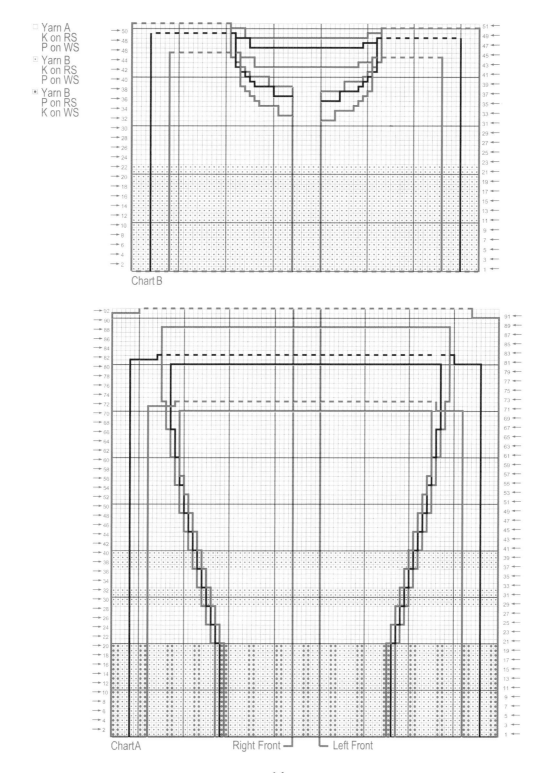

Yarn A
K on RS
P on WS

Yarn B
K on RS
P on WS

Yarn B
P on RS
K on WS

Chart B

Chart A

Right Front

Left Front

29

Bounce Sweater

Age	1-2 years	2-3 years	3-4 years

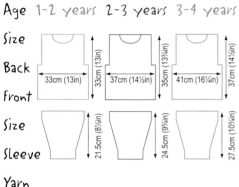

Size			
Back	33cm (13in) 33cm (13in)	37cm (14½in) 35cm (13¾in)	41cm (16¼in) 37cm (14½in)
Front			
Size	21.5cm (8½in)	24.5cm (9¾in)	27.5cm (10¾in)
Sleeve			

Yarn

Rowan Denim x 50g balls

A. Memphis	5	5	6
B. Ecru	2	3	3

Needles

1 pair 3 ¼ mm (US 3) needles for rib
1 pair 4 mm (US 6) needles for main body

Tension

20 sts and 28 rows to 10cm measured over stocking stitch using 4 mm (US 6) needles before washing

Back

Using 3 ¼ mm (US 3) needles and yarn A, cast on 66,74,82 sts and work from chart and written instructions as folls:
Chart row 1: K2,0,4, (P2,K4) 10,12,12 times, P2, K2,0,4.
Chart row 2: P2,0,4, (K2,P4) 10,12,12 times, K2, P2,0,4.
Cont in rib from chart until row 12 completed.
Change to 4 mm (US 6) needles and joining in and breaking off colours as indicated on chart work in patterned stocking stitch using the intarsia technique for ball motifs, until chart row 68,70,72 completed.
Shape armhole
Cast off 6 sts at the beg next 2 rows. (54,62,70 sts)
Work until chart row 108,114,120 completed.
Shape shoulders and back neck
Chart row 109,115,121: Patt 13,16,19 sts, turn and leave rem sts on a holder.
Chart row 110,116,122: Cast off 3 sts, patt to end.
Slip rem 10,13,16 sts onto a holder.
Slip centre 28,30,32 sts onto a holder, rejoin yarn and patt to end. (13,16,19 sts)
Work 1 row.
Chart row 111,117,123: Cast off 3 sts, patt to end.
Slip rem 10,13,16 sts onto a holder.

Front

Work as for back until chart row 98,104,110 completed.
Shape front neck
Chart row 99,105,111: Patt 18,21,24 sts, turn and leave rem sts on a holder.
Chart row 100,106,112: Cast off 4 sts, patt to end.
Dec 1 st at neck edge on next 4 rows. (10,13,16 sts)
Work without further shaping until chart row 110,116,122 completed.
Slip rem sts onto a holder.
Slip centre 18,20,22 sts onto a holder, rejoin yarn to rem sts and patt to end. (18,21,24 sts)
Patt 1 row.
Chart row 101,107,113: Cast off 4 sts, patt to end.
Dec 1 st at neck edge on next 4 rows. (10,13,16 sts)
Work without further shaping until chart row 111,117,123 completed.
Slip rem sts onto a holder.

Sleeves (both alike)

Using 3 ¼ mm (US 3) needles and yarn A, cast on 34,36,38 sts and work from chart and written instructions as folls:
Chart row 1: P0,1,2, (K4, P2) 5 times, K4, P0,1,2.
Chart row 2: K0,1,2, (P4, K2) 5 times, P4, K0,1,2.
Cont in rib from chart until row 12 completed.
Change to 4 mm (US 6) needles and joining in and breaking off colours as indicated on chart work in patterned stocking stitch using the intarsia technique for ball motifs at the same time inc at side edges as folls:.
Chart row 13: Inc into first st, knit to last st, inc into last st. (36,38,40 sts)
Chart row 14: Purl.
Cont in patt from chart shaping sides by inc as

indicated to 52,56,60 sts.
Work without further shaping until chart row 72,82,92 completed.
Cast off.

Neckband

Join right shoulder seam by knitting sts together on the WS of garment using yarn A, as shown in techniques guide, page 48.
Using 3 ¼ mm (US 3) needles and yarn A pick up and knit 14 sts down left front neck, knit across 18,20,22 sts on holder, pick up and knit 14 sts to shoulder and 3 sts down right back neck, knit across 28,30,32 sts on holder, pick up and knit 3 sts to shoulder. (80,84,88 sts)
Rib row 1 (WS row): K0,1,0, P2,4,2, (K2, P4) to last 0,1,2 sts, K0,1,2.
Rib row 2 (RS row): P0,1,2, (K4, P2) to last 2,5,2 sts, K2,4,2, P0,1,0.
Work these 2 rows 5 times more.
Cast off in rib.
Join Left shoulder seam.

Sew in all ends and wash pieces as described on page 27.
Complete sweater as shown in making up instructions page 48.

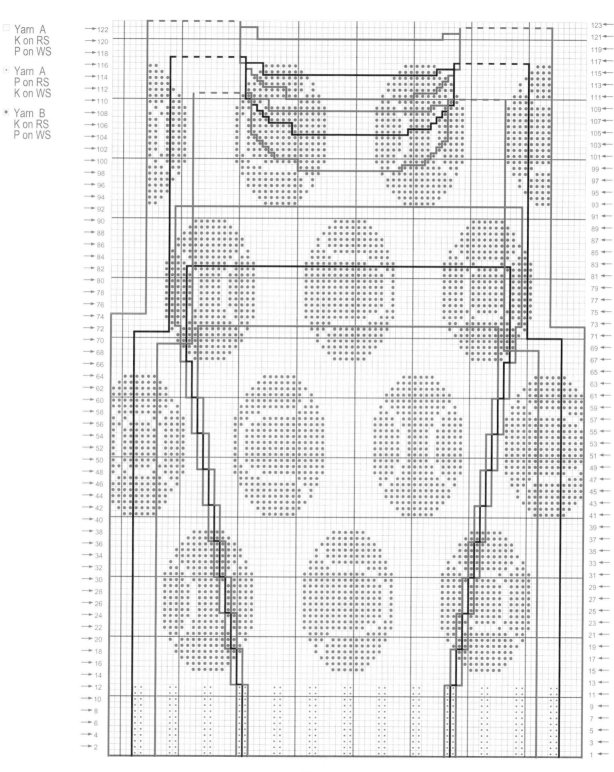

Target Slipover

Age 1-2 years 2-3 years 3-4 years

Size

Back

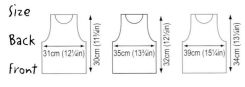

31cm (12¼in) 30cm (11¾in) 35cm (13¾in) 32cm (12½in) 39cm (15¼in) 34cm (13¼in)

Front

Yarn

Rowan Denim x 50g balls

A. Nashville	4	4	5
B. Memphis	1	1	1
C. Tennessee	1	1	1

Needles
1 pair 3 ¼ mm (US 3) needles for edging
1 pair 4 mm (US 6) needles for main body

Tension
20 sts and 28 rows to 10cm measured over stocking stitch using 4 mm (US 6) needles before washing

Note Target motif is worked on front only

Back
Using 3 ¼ mm (US 3) needles and yarn A, cast on 62,70,78 sts and work from chart and written instructions as folls:
Chart row 1: Knit.
Chart row 2: Purl.
Work these 2 rows twice more.
Change to 4 mm (US 6) needles and cont to work in stocking stitch only until chart row 62,68,68 completed.
Shape armhole
Cast off 4 sts at beginning next 2 rows.
(54,62,70 sts)

Dec 1 st at each end of next 3 rows and 2 foll alt rows. (44,52,60 sts)
Work 3 rows.
Dec 1 st at armhole edge on next row.
(42,50,58 sts)
Work without further shaping to chart row 102,110,114 completed.
Shape shoulders and back neck
Cast off 3,4,6 sts at the beg next row, knit until 6,8,9 sts on RH needle, turn and leave rem sts on a holder.
Chart row 104,112,116: Cast off 3 sts, purl to end.
Cast off rem 3,5,6 sts.
Slip centre 24,26,28 sts onto a holder, rejoin yarn to rem sts and knit to end. (9,12,15 sts)
Chart row 104,112,116: Cast off 3,4,6 sts, purl to end. (6,8,9 sts)
Chart row 105,113,117: Cast off 3 sts, knit to end.
Cast off rem 3,5,6 sts.

Front
Work as for back until chart row 20 completed.
Now using the intarsia method of joining in and breaking off new colours as required work central motif from chart as folls:
Chart row 21: K 25,29,33 sts using yarn A, join in yarn B and K 12 sts, join in another length of yarn A and K 25,29,33.
Chart row 22: P 23,27,31 sts using yarn A, P 16 sts using yarn B and P 23,27,31 sts using yarn A.
Cont to work from chart as for back working motif as indicated until chart row 92,100,104 completed.
Shape front neck
Chart row 93,101,105: K 14,17,20 sts, turn and leave rem sts on a holder.
Chart row 94,102,106: Cast off 4 sts, purl to end.
Dec 1 st at neck edge on next 4 rows. (6,9,12 sts)
Work without further shaping until chart row 102,110,114 completed.
Cast off 3,4,6 sts at beg next row.
Purl 1 row.
Cast off rem 3,5,6 sts.
Slip centre 14,16,18 sts onto a holder, rejoin yarn to rem sts and knit to end. (14,17,20 sts)
Purl 1 row.
Chart row 95,103,107: Cast off 4 sts, knit to end.
Dec 1 st at neck edge on next 4 rows. (6,9,12 sts)
Work without further shaping to chart row 103,111,115 completed
Shape shoulder
Cast off 3,4,6 sts at beg next row.
Knit 1 row.
Cast off rem 3,5,6 sts.

Join right shoulder seam using backstitch.

Neck Edging
With RS facing and using 3 ¼ mm (US 3) needles and yarn A pick up and knit 14 sts down left front neck, knit across 14,16,18, sts from front neck holder, pick up and knit 14 sts to shoulder and 3 sts down right back neck, knit across 24,26,28 sts from back neck holder, pick up and knit 3 sts to shoulder. (72,76,80 sts)
Beg with a P row work 7 rows in st st.
Cast off.
Join left shoulder seam using backstitch.

Armhole edging (both alike)
With RS facing and using 3 ¼ mm (US 3) needles and yarn A pick up and knit 30,32,35 sts from side seam to shoulder and 30,32,35 sts down to side seam. (60,64,70 sts)
Knit 2 rows.
Cast off knitwise.

Sew in all ends and wash pieces as described on page 27.
Complete slipover as shown in making up instructions on page 48.

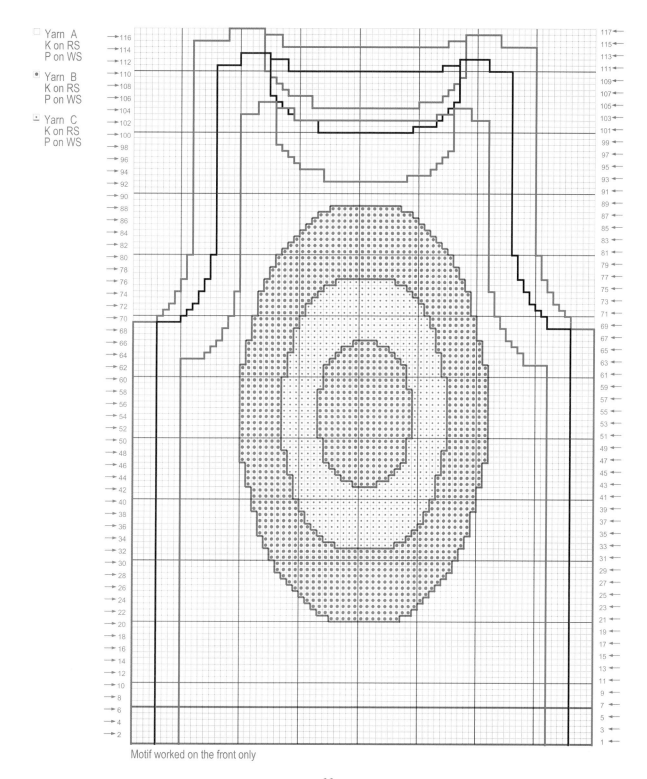

Yarn A
K on RS
P on WS

Yarn B
K on RS
P on WS

Yarn C
K on RS
P on WS

Motif worked on the front only

Polly Pocket Dress

Age 1-2 years   2-3 years   3-4 years

Size

Back

Front

27cm (10¾in)   30cm (11¾in)   33cm (13in)

45cm (17¼in)   48cm (19in)   51cm (20½in)

39cm (15¼in)   42cm (16½in)   45cm (17¾in)

Yarn
Rowan Denim x 50g balls

A. Nashville	5	6	6
B. Tennessee	1	1	1

Needles
1 pair 3 ¼ mm (US 3) needles for edging
1 pair 4 mm (US 6) needles for main body

Button 1

Tension
20 sts and 28 rows to 10cm measured over stocking stitch using 4 mm (US 6) needles before washing

Back
Using 3 ¼ mm (US 3) needles and yarn A, cast on 79,85,91 sts and work from chart and written instructions as folls:
Chart row 1: K1,0,1, (P1, K1) to last 0,1,0 st, P0,1,0.
Chart row 2: K1,0,1, (P1, K1) to last 0,1,0 st, P0,1,0.
Cont in moss st until chart row 6 completed.
Change to 4 mm (US 6) needles work in st st until chart row 16 completed.
Row 17 (dec): K2tog, knit to last 2 sts, K2tog. (77,83,89 sts)
Work 7 rows in st st beg with a purl row.

Dec as above at beg and end next row and every foll 8th row to 55,61,67 sts.
Work without further shaping until row 114,118,126 completed.

Shape armhole and divide for back neck
Chart row 115,119,127: Cast off 4 sts at the beg next row, knit until there are 23,26,29 sts on RH needle, turn and leave rem sts on a holder.
Work each side of neck separately.
Chart row 116,120,128: Purl.
Chart row 117,121,129: Cast off 3 sts at the beg next row, knit to end.
Chart row 118,122,130: Purl.
Dec 1 st at armhole edge on next 3 rows and 2 foll alt rows. (15,18,21 sts)
Work without further shaping until row 145,153,163 completed.

Shape back neck
Chart row 146,154,164: Cast off 8,9,10 sts, purl to end. (7,9,11 sts)
Dec 1 st at neck edge on next 3 rows. (4,6,8 sts)
Purl 1 row. Cast off rem sts.
Slip centre st onto a holder, rejoin yarn to rem sts, knit to end. (27,30,33 sts)
Chart row 116,120,128: Cast off 4 sts at the beg next row, purl to end.
Knit 1 row.
Chart row 118,122,130: Cast off 3 sts at the beg next row, purl to end.
Dec 1 st at armhole edge on next 3 rows and 2 foll alt rows. (15,18,21 sts)
Work without further shaping until row 146,154,164 completed.

Shape back neck
Chart row 147,155,165: Cast off 8,9,10 sts, knit to end. (7,9,11 sts)
Dec 1 sts at neck edge on next 3 rows. (4,6,8 sts)
Cast off rem sts.

Front
Work as for back until chart row 114,118,126 completed.
Shape armhole
Cast off 4 sts at beginning next 2 rows and 3 sts at beg foll 2 rows. (41,47,53 sts)
Dec 1 st at each end of next 3 rows and 2 foll alt rows. (31,37,43 sts)
Work without further shaping to chart row 138,146,156 completed.
Shape front neck
Chart row 139,147,157: Knit 10,12,14 sts, turn and leave rem sts on a holder.
Chart row 140,148,158: cast off 4 sts, purl to end.

Dec 1 st at neck edge on next 2 rows. (4,6,8 sts)
Work without further shaping until chart row 150,158,168 completed.
Cast off rem sts.
Slip centre 11,13,15 sts onto a holder, rejoin yarn to rem sts, knit to end.
Purl 1 row.
Chart row 141,149,159: Cast off 4 sts, knit to end.
Dec 1 st at neck edge on next 2 rows.
(4,6,8 sts)
Work without further shaping until chart row 150,158,168 completed.
Cast off rem sts.

Patch Pockets (work 2)
Using 4 mm (US 6) needles cast on 25 sts and yarn A and work from chart for pocket as folls:
Chart row 1: (K1, P1) to last st, K1.
Chart row 2: (K1, P1) to last st, K1.
Work these 2 rows once more.
Chart row 5: K1, P1, K21, P1, K1.
Chart row 6: K1, P1, K1, P19, K1, P1, K1.
Work these 2 rows once more.
Chart row 9: K1,P1, K7 sts using yarn A, join in yarn B and K 2 sts, join in another length of yarn A and K 12, P1, K1.
Chart row 10: K1, P1, K1, P4 sts using yarn A, P2 sts using yarn B, P4 sts using yarn A, P4 using yarn B change to yarn A P5, K1, P1, K1.
Cont to work from pocket chart as indicated until chart row 38 completed.
Cast off sts.

Back neck opening
With RS facing and using 3 ¼ mm (US 3) needles and yarn A, pick up and K19,21,23 sts down right back neck opening, K 1 st from centre back neck holder and 19,21,23 sts up left back neck opening. (39,43,47 sts)
Cast off knitwise 18,20,22 slip1, K2tog, psso, cast off all rem sts.
Join both shoulder seams using backstitch.

Neck edging
With RS facing and using 3 ¼ mm (US 3) needles and yarn A, and starting at centre back pick up and knit 11,12,13 sts to shoulder, 11 sts down left front neck, 11,13,15 sts from front neck holder, pick up and knit 11 sts to shoulder, and 11,12,13 sts to centre back (55,59,63 sts)
Work 2 rows in moss st setting sts as for back.
Cast off knitwise on WS row.

Armhole edgings (both alike)

With RS facing and using 3 ¼ mm (US 3) needles and yarn A, pick up and knit 29,31,32 sts from side seam to shoulder and 29,31,32 sts down to side seam. (58,62,64 sts)

Row 1: (K1, P1) to end.
Row 2: (P1, K1) to end.
Cast off knitwise on WS row.

Making up

Make a button loop at top opening on right back, sew button on left side to match.

Sew in all ends and wash pieces as described on page 27.

Sew pockets to front, postioning centrally and 11,12,13 cm up from cast on edge.

☐ Yarn A
K on RS
P on WS

⊡ Yarn A
P on RS
K on WS

⊙ Yarn B
K on RS
P on WS

Pocket chart

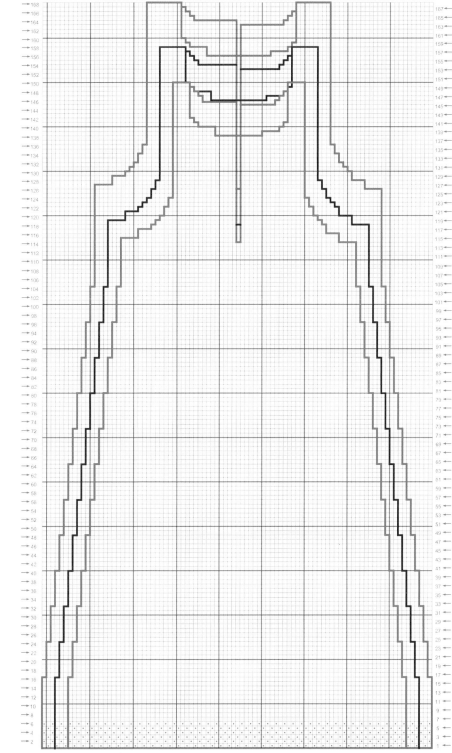

35

Sand castle Sweater

Age 1-2 years 2-3 years 3-4 years

Size

Back

Front

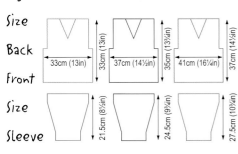

Size

Sleeve

Yarn
Rowan Denim x 50g balls

Tennessee	6	7	7

Needles
1 pair 3 ¼ mm (US 3) needles for edging
1 pair 4 mm (US 6) needles for main body

Tension
20 sts and 28 rows to 10cm measured over pattern using 4 mm (US 6) needles before washing

Back
Using 3 ¼ mm (US 3) needles cast on 66,74,82 sts and work from chart and written instructions as folls:
Chart row 1: Knit.
Chart row 2: Purl.
Work these 2 rows twice more.
Change to 4 mm (US 6) needles and cont to work in patt as indicated on chart until chart row 70,72,74 completed.
Shape armhole
Cast off 6 sts at the beg next 2 rows. (54,62,70 sts)
Work until chart row 112,118,124 completed.

Shape shoulders and back neck
Cast off 4,5,6 sts at the beg next 2 rows.
Chart row 115,121,127: Cast off 4,5,6 sts, patt until 8,9,10 sts on RH needle, turn and leave rem sts on a holder.
Chart row 116,122,128: Cast off 3 sts, patt to end. Cast off rem 5,6,7 sts.
Slip centre 22,24,26 sts onto a holder, rejoin yarn to rem sts and patt to end. (12,14,16 sts)
Chart row 116,122,128: Cast off 4,5,6 sts, patt to end. (8,9,10 sts)
Chart row 117,123,129: Cast off 3 sts, patt to end. Cast off rem 5,6,7 sts.

Front
Work as for back until chart row 84,88,92 completed.
Shape front neck
Chart row 85,89,93: Patt 26,30,34 sts, turn and leave rem sts on a holder.
Work 1 row.
Chart row 87,91,95: Patt to last 2 sts, K2tog.
Work 1 row.
Cont to dec as indicated at front neck until 13,16,19 sts rem.
Work until chart row 112,118,124 completed.
Shape shoulder
Cast off 4,5,6 sts at beg next row and foll alt row.
Work 1 row.
Cast off rem 5,6,7 sts.
Slip centre 2 sts onto a holder, rejoin yarn to rem sts and knit to end. (26,30,34 sts)
Work 1 row.
Chart row 87,91,95: K2tog, patt to end.
Work 1 row.
Cont to dec as indicated at front neck until 13,16,19 sts rem.
Work until chart row 113,119,125 completed.
Shape shoulder
Cast off 4,5,6 sts at beg next row and foll alt row.
Work 1 row.
Cast off rem 5,6,7 sts.

Sleeves (both alike)
Using 3 ¼ mm (US 3) needles cast on 34,36,38 sts and work from chart and written instructions as folls:
Chart row 1: Knit.
Chart row 2: Purl.
Work these 2 rows twice more.
Change to 4 mm (US 6) needles and cont to work in patt as indicated on chart until row 10 completed.
Chart row 11: Inc into first st, patt to last st, inc into last st. (36,38,40 sts)

Chart row 12: Patt across row.
Cont in patt from chart, shaping sides by inc as indicated to 52,56,60 sts.
Work without further shaping until chart row 74,84,94 completed.
Cast off.

Neckband
Join right shoulder seam using backstitch.
With RS facing and using 3 ¼ mm (US 3) needles pick up and knit 26,28,30 sts down left front neck, knit across 2 sts on holder, pick up and knit 26,28,30 sts to shoulder and 3 sts down right back neck, pick up and knit across 22,24,26 sts at centre back, pick up and knit 3 sts to shoulder. (82,88,94 sts)
Edging row 1 (WS row): Purl.
Edging row 2 (RS row): K25,27,29, K2tog tbl, K2tog,K53,57,61. (80,86,92 sts)
Edging row 3: Purl.
Edging row 4: K24,26,28, K2tog tbl, K2tog, K52,56,60. (78,84,90 sts)
Edging row 5: Purl.
Edging row 6: K23,25,27, K2tog tbl, K2tog, K51,55,59 (76,82,88 sts)
Cast off rem sts.
Join left shoulder seam and neckband using backstitch.

Sew in all ends and wash pieces as described on page 27.
Complete sweater as shown in making up instructions page 48.

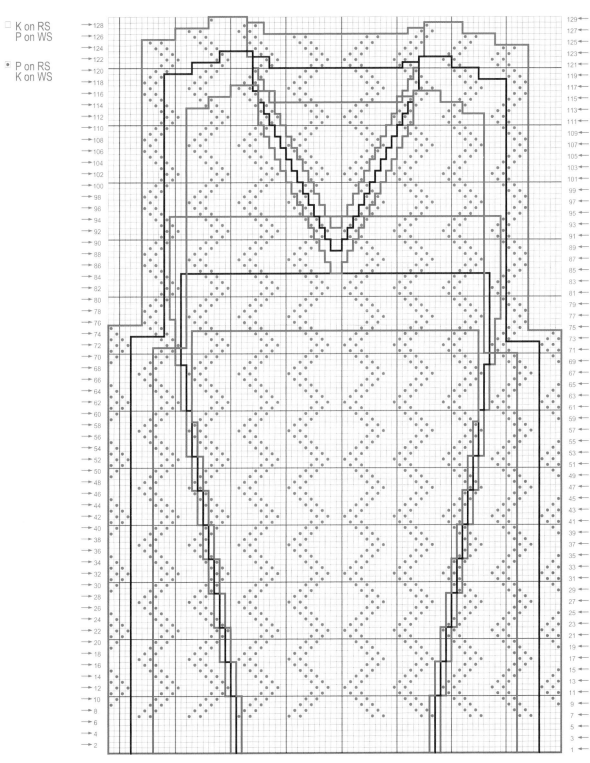

Breeze Sweater

Age   1-2 years   2-3 years   3-4 years

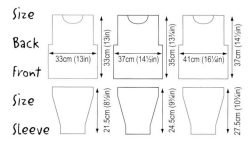

Yarn
Rowan Denim x 50g balls
Nashville   6   6   7

Needles
1 pair 3 ¼ mm (US 3) needles for rib
1 pair 4 mm (US 6) needles for main body

Tension
20 sts and 28 rows to 10cm measured over stocking stitch using 4 mm (US 6) needles before washing

Back
Using 3 ¼ mm (US 3) needles cast on 67,75,83 sts and work from chart and written instructions as folls:
Chart row 1: K3,1,5 (P1, K5) 10,12,12 times, P1, K3,1,5.
Chart row 2: P2,0,4 (K1, P1, K1, P3) 10,12,12 times, K1, P1, K1, P2,0,4.
Cont in rib from chart until row 20 completed.
Change to 4 mm (US 6) needles work in st st only until chart row 68,70,72 completed.
Shape armhole
Cast off 6 sts at the beg next 2 rows. (55,63,71 sts)
Work until chart row 110,116,122 completed.

Shape shoulders and back neck
Cast off 4,5,6 sts at the beg next 2 rows.
Chart row 113,119,125: Cast off 4,5,6, sts, knit until 7,8,9 sts on RH needle, turn and leave rem sts on a holder.
Chart row 114,120,126: Cast off 3 sts, purl to end. Cast off rem 4,5,6 sts.
Slip centre 25,27,29 sts onto a holder, rejoin yarn to rem sts and knit to end. (11,13,15 sts)
Chart row 114,120,126: Cast off 4,5,6 purl to end. (7,8,9 sts)
Chart row 115,121,127: Cast off 3 sts, knit to end. Cast off rem 4,5,6 sts.

Front
Work as for back until chart row 102,108,114 completed.
Shape front neck
Chart row 103,109,115: Knit 20,23,26 sts, turn and leave rem sts on a holder.
Chart row 104,110,116: Cast off 4 sts, purl to end.
Dec 1 st at neck edge on next 4 rows. (12,15,18 sts)
Work without further shaping until chart row 110,116,122 completed.
Shape shoulder
Cast off 4,5,6 sts at beg next row and foll alt row.
Purl 1 row.
Cast off rem 4,5,6 sts.
Slip centre 15,17,19 sts onto a holder, rejoin yarn to rem sts and knit to end. (20,23,26 sts)
Purl 1 row.
Chart row 105,111,117: Cast off 4 sts, knit to end.
Dec 1 st at neck edge on next 4 rows. (12,15,18 sts)
Work without further shaping until chart row 111,117,123 completed.
Shape shoulder
Cast off 4,5,6 sts at beg next row and foll alt row.
Knit 1 row.
Cast off rem 4,5,6 sts.

Sleeves (both alike)
Using 3 ¼ mm (US 3) needles cast on 35,37,39 sts and work from chart and written instructions as folls:
Chart row 1: K5,0,1 (P1, K5) 4,6,6 times, P1, K5,0,1.
Chart row 2: K0,0,1 P0,1,1, K1, (P3, K1, P1, K1) 5,5,6 times, P3,3,0, K1,1,0, P0,1,0.
Cont in rib from chart until row 20 completed.
Change to 4 mm (US 6) needles and work in st st only.
Chart row 21: Inc into first st, knit to last st, inc into last st. (37,39,41 sts)
Chart row 22: Purl.
Cont in patt from chart shaping sides by inc as

indicated to 53,57,61 sts.
Work without further shaping until chart row 72,82,92 completed.
Cast off.

Neckband
Join right shoulder seam using backstitch.
Using 3 ¼ mm (US 3) needles and pick up and knit 14 sts down left front neck, knit across 15,17,19 sts on holder, pick up and knit 14 sts to shoulder and 3 sts down right back neck, knit across 25,27,29 sts or holder, pick up and knit 3 sts to shoulder. (74,78,82 sts)
Rib row 1 (WS row): P4,1,4, (K1, P5) 11,12,12 times, K1, P3,4,5.
Rib row 2 (RS row): P0,0,1, K2,3,3, (P1, K1, P1, K3) 12,12,13 times, P0,1,0, K0,1,0, P0,1,0.
Work these 2 rows 4 times more.
Cast off in rib.
Join left shoulder and neckband seam.

Sew in all ends and wash pieces as described on page 27.
Complete sweater as shown in making up instructions page 48.

K on RS
P on WS

P on RS
K on WS

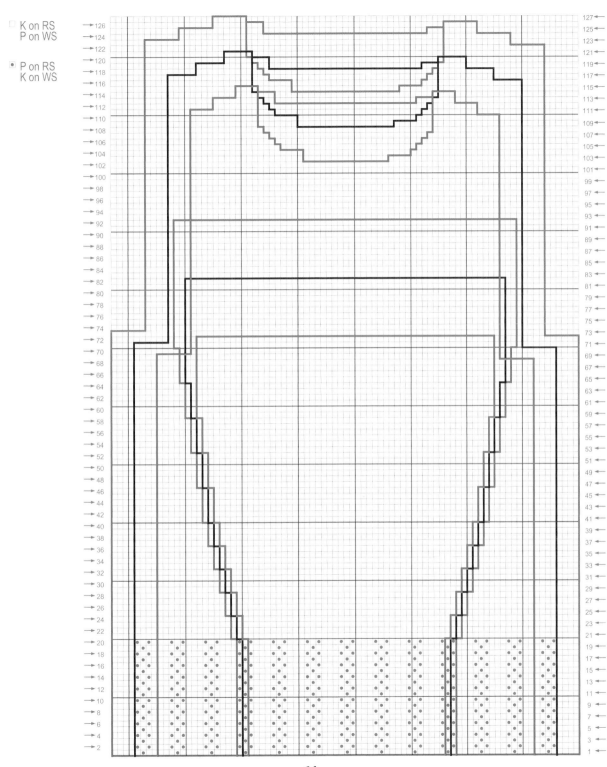

39

Tide Cardigan

Age 1-2 years   2-3 years   3-4 years

Size

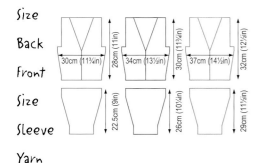

Back

Front

30cm (11¾in)   34cm (13½in)   37cm (14¼in)
28cm (11in)   30cm (11¾in)   32cm (12½in)

Size

Sleeve

22.5cm (9in)   26cm (10¼in)   29cm (11½in)

Yarn
Rowan Denim x 50g balls
A. Tennessee   5   5   6

Needles
1 pair 3 ¼ mm (US 3) needles for edging
1 pair 4 mm (US 6) needles for main body

Buttons 5

Tension
20 sts and 28 rows to 10cm measured over st st using
4 mm (US 6) needles before washing

Back
Using 3 ¼ mm (US 3) needles work picot cast on as
follows:
*Cast on 5 sts, cast off 2 sts slip st on RH needle back
onto LH needle* (3 sts now on LH needle) rep from
* to * until 57,66,75 sts on needle, Cast on 2,1,0 sts.
(59,67,75 sts)
Knit 2 rows.
Work lace pattern as folls:
Row 3: K2,2,3 (yo, k2tog tbl, K1) 1,0,1 time (K1, K2tog,

---

yo, K1, yo, K2tog tbl, K1) 7,9,9 times, (K1, K2tog, yo,)
1,0,1 time, K2,2,3.
Row 4: Purl.
Row 5: K3,2,4 (yo, k2tog tbl,) 1,0,1 time (K2tog, yo,
K3, yo, K2tog tbl) 7,9,9 times, (K2tog, yo,) 1,0,1 time,
K3,2,4.
Row 6: Purl.
Change to 4 mm (US 6) needles and work 4 rows of
lace pattern 3 more times as above.
Row 19: Knit.
Row 20: Purl.
Now working from chart starting at row 1 work in st st
only until chart row 30,32,36 completed.
Shape armhole
Cast off 6 sts at the beg next 2 rows.
(47,55,63 sts)
Work until chart row 72,78,86 completed.
Shape shoulders and back neck
Cast off 4,5,6 sts at the beg next 2 rows.
Chart row 75,81,89: Cast off 4,5,6 sts, knit until
7,8,9 sts on RH needle, turn and leave rem sts on
a holder.
Chart row 76,82,90: Cast off 3 sts, purl to end.
Cast off rem 4,5,6 sts.
Rejoin yarn and cast off centre 17,19,21 sts, knit to end.
(11,13,15 sts)
Chart row 76,82,90: Cast off 4,5,6 sts, purl to end.
(7,8,9 sts)
Chart row 77,83,91: Cast off 3 sts, knit to end.
Cast off rem 4,5,6 sts.

Left Front
Using 3 ¼ mm (US 3) needles work picot cast on as
follows:
*Cast on 5 sts, cast off 2 sts slip st on RH needle back
onto LH needle* (3 sts now on LH needle) rep from
* to * until 30,33,36 sts on needle, Cast on 0,1,2 sts.
(30,34,38 sts)
Knit 2 rows.
Work lace pattern as folls:
Row 3: K2,2,3 (yo, k2tog tbl, K1) 1,0,1 time (K1, K2tog,
yo, K1, yo, K2tog tbl, K1) 3,4,4 times, K1, K2tog, yo, K1.
Row 4: Purl.
Row 5: K3,2,4 (yo, k2tog tbl,) 1,0,1 time (K2tog, yo, K3,
yo, K2tog tbl) 3,4,4 times, K2tog, yo, K2.
Row 6: Purl.
Change to 4 mm (US 6) needles and work 4 rows of
lace pattern 3 more times as above.
Row 19: Knit.
Row 20: Purl.
Now working from chart starting at row 1 work in st st
only until chart row 30,32,36 completed.

Shape armhole and front neck
Cast off 6 sts at the beg next row, patt to last 2 sts,
K2tog. (23,27,31 sts)
Cont to dec at neck edge as indicated to 12,15,18 sts.
Work without further shaping until chart row
72,78,86 completed.
Shape shoulder
Cast off 4,5,6 sts at the beg next row and foll alt row.
Work 1 row.
Cast off rem 4,5,6 sts.

Right Front
Using 3 ¼ mm (US 3) needles work picot cast on as
follows:
*Cast on 5 sts, cast off 2 sts slip st on RH needle bac
onto LH needle* (3 sts now on LH needle) rep from
* to * until 30,33,36 sts on needle, Cast on 0,1,2 sts.
(30,34,38 sts)
Knit 2 rows.
Work lace pattern as folls:
Row 3: K1, yo, k2tog tbl, K1, (K1, K2tog, yo, K1, yo,
K2tog tbl, K1) 3,4,4 times, (K1, K2tog, yo) 1,0,1 time,
K2,2,3.
Row 4: Purl.
Row 5: K2, yo, k2tog tbl, (K2tog, yo, K3, yo, K2tog tb
3,4,4 times, (K2tog, yo) 1,0,1 time, K3,2,4.
Row 6: Purl.
Change to 4 mm (US 6) needles and work 4 rows of
lace pattern 3 more times as above.
Complete to match left front, foll chart for right front
and reversing shaping.

Sleeves (both alike)
Using 3 ¼ mm (US 3) needles work picot cast on as
follows:
*Cast on 5 sts, cast off 2 sts slip st on RH needle bac
onto LH needle* (3 sts now on LH needle) rep from
* to * until 33,36,39 sts on needle, Cast on 2,1,0 sts.
(35,37,39 sts)
Knit 2 rows.
Work lace pattern as folls:
Row 3: K0,1,2 (K1, K2tog, yo, K1, yo, K2tog tbl, K1)
5 times, K0,1,2.
Row 4: Purl.
Row 5: K0,1,2 (K2tog, yo, K3, yo, K2tog tbl) 5 times,
K0,1,2.
Row 6: Purl.
Change to 4 mm (US 6) needles and work 4 rows of
lace pattern 3 more times as above.
Row 19: Inc into first st, knit to last st, inc into last st.
(37,39,41 sts)
Row 20: Purl.

nt from chart, shaping sides
inc as indicated on chart to
55,59 sts.
rk without further shaping
til chart row 54,66,76
mpleted. Cast off.

ontband
n both shoulder seams
ng backstitch.
th RS of right front facing
d using 3 ¼ mm (US 3)
edles, pick up and knit
,32,36 sts from cast
edge to start of neck
aping, 26,28,30 sts up
ht front neck slope to
oulder, 23,25,27 sts across
ck neck, pick up and knit
,28,30 sts down left front
ck slope, and 32,32,36 sts
end. (139,145, 159 sts)
xt row: Knit.
ttonhole row (RS): K1,
tog, yo, (K5,5,6, K2tog, yo)
mes, knit to end.
t 2 rows.
rk picot cast off as folls:
st off 3 sts, *slip st on RH
edle back onto LH needle,
st on 2 sts using the cable
thod, then cast off 5 sts,
from * to end.

w in all ends and wash
ces as on page 27.
mplete cardigan as shown
making up instructions,
ge 48.
w on buttons to correspond
h buttonholes.

☐ K on RS
P on WS

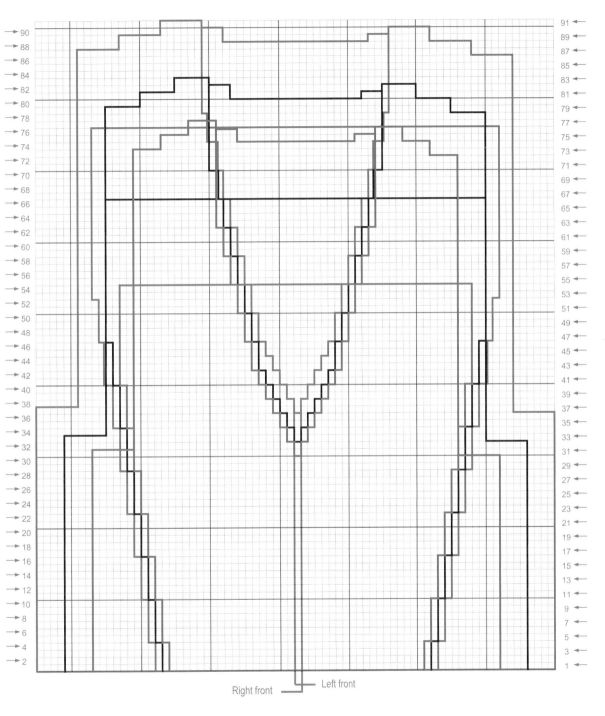

Right front   Left front

Rope Sweater

Age 1-2 years   2-3 years   3-4 years

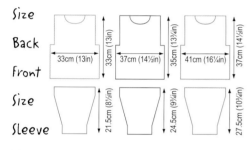

	Size	Back	Front
	33cm (13in)	33cm (13in)	
	37cm (14½in)		
	35cm (13¾in)	41cm (16¼in)	37cm (14½in)

Size Sleeve: 21.5cm (8½in) 24.5cm (9¾in) 27.5cm (10¾in)

Yarn
Rowan Denim x 50g balls
Ecru   6   7   7

Needles
1 pair 3 ¼ mm (US 3) needles for rib
1 pair 4 mm (US 6) needles for main body

Tension
20 sts and 28 rows to 10cm measured over stocking stitch using 4 mm (US 6) needles before washing

Note
The chart is for the sweater front only, work from written instructions for back and sleeves, using chart as a guide for back as shaping and rows are the same.

Front
Using 3 ¼ mm (US 3) needles cast on 66,74,82 sts and work from chart and written instructions as folls:
Chart row 1: K2,1,0, (P2, K3) 4,5,6 times, P2, K4, P1, K8, P1, K4, P2, (K3 P2) 4,5,6 times, K2,1,0.
Chart row 2: P2,1,0, (K2, P3) 4,5,6 times, K2, P3, K1, P1, K1, P6, K1, P1, K1, P3, K2, (P3 K2) 4,5,6 times,

P2,1,0.
Cont in rib from chart until row 4 completed.
Work row 1 once more.
Chart row 6 (inc): P2,1,0, (K2, P3) 4,5,6 times, K2, P2, M1P, P1, K1, P1, K1, (P2, M1P)twice, P2, (K1, P1) twice, M1P, P2, K2, (P3, K2) 4,5,6 times, P2,1,0. (70,78,86 sts)
Chart row 7: K2,1,0, (P2, K3) 4,5,6 times, P2, C4F, K1, P1, K1, C8B, K1, P1, K1, C4B, P2, (K3 P2) 4,5,6 times, K2,1,0.
Chart row 8: P2,1,0, (K2, P3) 4,5,6 times, K2, P4, K1, P1, K1, P8, K1, P1, K1, P4, K2, (P3 K2) 4,5,6 times, P2,1,0.
Chart row 9: K2,1,0, (P2, K3) 4,5,6 times, P2, K5, P1, K10, P1, K5, P2, (K3 P2) 4,5,6 times, K2,1,0.
Chart row 10: As row 8.
Chart row 11: As row 9.
Chart row 12: As row 8.
Change to 4 mm (US 6) needles and work in st st and cable panel as indicated on chart until row 68,70,72 completed.

Shape armhole
Cast off 6 sts at the beg next 2 rows. (58,66,74 sts)
Work until chart row 102,108,114 completed.

Shape front neck
Chart row 103,109,115: Patt 19,22,25 sts, turn and leave rem sts on a holder.
Chart row 104,110,116: Cast off 4 sts, purl to end.
Dec 1 st at neck edge on next 4 rows. (11,14,17 sts)
Work without further shaping to chart row 110,116,122.

Shape shoulder
Cast off 4,5,6 sts at beg next row and foll alt row.
Purl 1 row.
Cast off rem 3,4,5 sts.
Slip centre 20,22,24 sts onto a holder, rejoin yarn to rem sts and patt to end. (19,22,25 sts)
Purl 1 row.
Chart row 105,111,117: Cast off 4 sts, knit to end.
Dec 1 st at neck edge on next 4 rows. (11,14,17 sts)
Work without further shaping to chart row 111,117,123.

Shape shoulder
Cast off 4,5,6 sts at beg next row and foll alt row.
Knit 1 row.
Cast off rem 3,4,5 sts.

Back
Using 3 ¼ mm (US 3) needles cast on 66,74,82 sts and work from written instructions as folls:
Row 1: K2,1,0, (P2, K3) 12,14,16 times, P2, K2,1,0.
Row 2: P2,1,0, (K2, P3) 12,14,16 times, K2, P2,1,0.
Cont in rib until 12 rows in all completed.
Change to 4 mm (US 6) needles and work in st st until

68,70,72 rows in all completed.
Shape armhole
Cast off 6 sts at the beg next 2 rows. (54,62,70 sts)
Work until 110,116,122 rows in all completed.
Shape shoulders and back neck
Cast off 4,5,6 sts at the beg next 2 rows.
Row 113,119,125: Cast off 4,5,6 sts, knit until 6,7,8 st on RH needle, turn and leave rem sts on a holder.
Row 114,120,126: Cast off 3 sts, purl to end.
Cast off rem 3,4,5 sts.
Slip centre 26,28,30 sts onto a holder, rejoin yarn to rem sts and knit to end. (10,12,14 sts)
Row 114,120,126: Cast off 4,5,6 sts, purl to end. (6,7,8 sts)
Row 115,121,127: Cast off 3 sts, knit to end.
Cast off rem sts.

Sleeves (both alike)
Using 3 ¼ mm (US 3) needles cast on 34,36,38 sts a work from written instructions as folls:
Row 1: K1,2,3 (P2, K3) 6 times, P2, K1,2,3.
Row 2: P1,2,3 (K2, P3) 6 times, K2, P1,2,3.
Cont in rib until 12 rows in all completed.
Change to 4 mm (US 6) needles and work in st st on
Row 13: Inc into first st, knit to last st, inc into last st. (36,38,40 sts)
Row 14: Purl.
Work 4 rows in st st.
Inc at each end of next row and every foll 6th row to 52,56,60 sts.
Work without further shaping until 72,82,92 rows in a completed.
Cast off.

Neckband
Join right shoulder seam using backstitch.
Using 3 ¼ mm (US 3) needles and pick up and knit 11 sts down left front neck, Work across 20,22,24 sts on front neck holder as folls: K6,7,8, K2tog, K4, K2tog K6,7,8, pick up and knit 11 sts to shoulder and 3 sts down right back neck, knit across 26,28,30 sts on holder, pick up and knit 3 sts to shoulder. (72,76,80 s
Rib row 1 (WS row): K2, P2 to end.
Rib row 2 (RS row): K2, P2 to end.
Work these 2 rows 6 times more.
Cast off in rib.
Join left shoulder and neckband seam.

Sew in all ends and wash pieces as described on page 27.
Complete sweater as shown in making up instruction page 48.

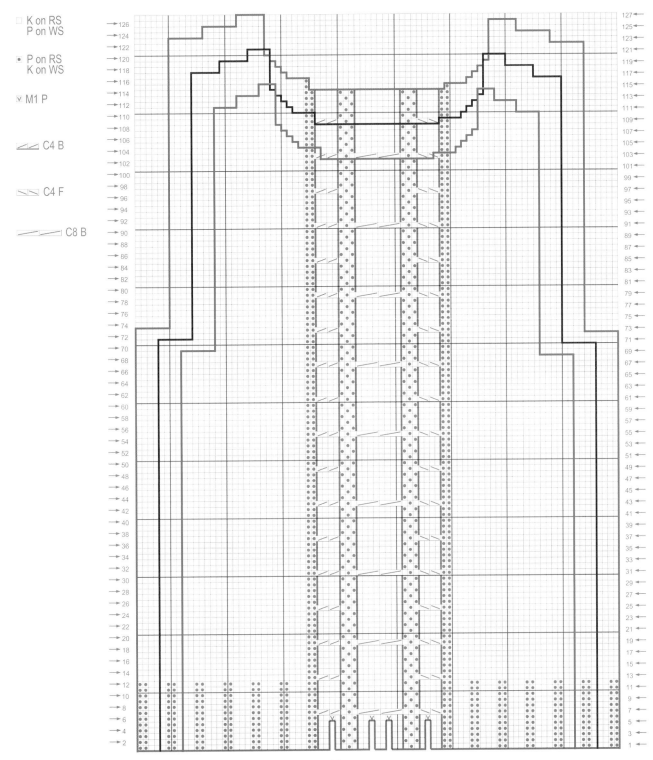

K on RS
P on WS

• P on RS
K on WS

v M1 P

C4 B

C4 F

C8 B

43

Seashore Sweater

Age 1-2 years 2-3 years 3-4 years

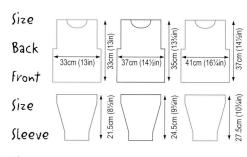

Yarn

Rowan Denim x 50g balls

A. Ecru	7	7	7
B. Nashville	1	1	2
C. Tennessee	1	1	1

Needles

1 pair 3 ¼ mm (US 3) needles for edging
1 pair 4 mm (US 6) needles for main body

Tension

20 sts and 28 rows to 10cm measured over stocking stitch using 4 mm (US 6) needles before washing

Back

Using 3 ¼ mm (US 3) needles and yarn A cast on 67,75,83 sts and work from chart and written instructions as folls:
Chart row 1: K1, P1, to last st K1.
Chart row 2: K1, P1, to last st K1.
Cont in moss st until chart row 8 completed.
Change to 4 mm (US 6) needles and using the intarsia method of joining in and breaking off new colours as required work from chart until chart row 68,70,72 completed.

Shape armhole
Cast off 6 sts at the beg next 2 rows. (55,63,71 sts)
Work until chart row 110,116,122 completed.

Shape shoulders and back neck
Cast off 4,5,6 sts at beg next 2 rows.
Chart row 113,119,125: Cast off 4,5,6 sts, knit until 7,8,9 sts on RH needle, turn and leave rem sts on a holder.
Chart row 114,120,126: Cast off 3 sts, purl to end.
Cast off rem 4,5,6 sts.
Slip centre 25,27,29 sts onto a holder, rejoin yarn to rem sts and knit to end. (11,13,15 sts)
Chart row 114,120,126: Cast off 4,5,6 sts, purl to end.
Chart row 115,121,127: Cast off 3 sts, knit to end.
Cast off rem 4,5,6 sts.

Front

Work as for back until chart row 102,108,114 completed.

Shape front neck
Chart row 103,109,115: Knit 20,23,26 sts, turn and leave rem sts on a holder.
Chart row 104,110,116: Cast off 4 sts, purl to end.
Dec 1 st at neck edge on next 4 rows. (12,15,18 sts)
Work without further shaping until chart row 110,116,122 completed.
Cast off 4,5,6 sts at beg next row and foll alt row.
Work 1 row.
Cast off rem 4,5,6 sts.
Slip centre 15,17,19 sts onto a holder, rejoin yarn to rem sts and knit to end. (20,23,26 sts)
Chart row 104,110,116: Purl 1 row.
Chart row 105,111,117: Cast off 4 sts, knit to end.
Dec 1 st at neck edge on next 4 rows. (12,15,18 sts)
Work without further shaping until chart row 111,117,123 completed.

Shape shoulder
Cast off 4,5,6 sts at beg next row and foll alt row.
Work 1 row.
Cast off rem 4,5,6 sts.

Sleeves (both alike)

Note do not work incomplete butterfly motif at top of sleeve.
Using 3 ¼ mm (US 3) needles and yarn A cast on 33,35,37 sts and work from chart and written instructions as folls:
Chart row 1: P1,0,1 (K1, P1) 16,17,18 times, K0,1,0.
Chart row 2: P1,0,1 (K1, P1) 16,17,18 times, K0,1,0.
Cont in moss st until chart row 8 completed.
Change to 4 mm (US 6) needles and and using the

intarsia method of joining in and breaking off new colours as required work from chart.
Chart row 9: Inc into first st, knit to last st, inc into last st. (35,37,39 sts)
Chart row 10: Purl.
Cont from chart, shaping sides by inc as indicated to 53,57,61 sts.
Work without further shaping until chart row 72,82,92 completed.
Cast off.

Neckband

Join right shoulder using backstitch.
Using 3 ¼ mm (US 3) needles and yarn A pick up and knit 13 sts down left front neck, knit across 15,17,19 sts on holder, pick up and knit 13 sts to shoulder and 3 sts down right back neck, knit across 25,27,29 sts on holder and pick up and knit 3 sts to shoulder. (72,76,80 sts)
Edging row 1 (WS): K1,P1 to end.
Edging row 2: P1,K1 to end.
Work these 2 rows twice more.
Cast off knitwise.
Join left shoulder and neck edging using back stitch.

Sew in all ends and wash pieces as described on page 27.
Complete sweater as shown in making up instruction page 48.

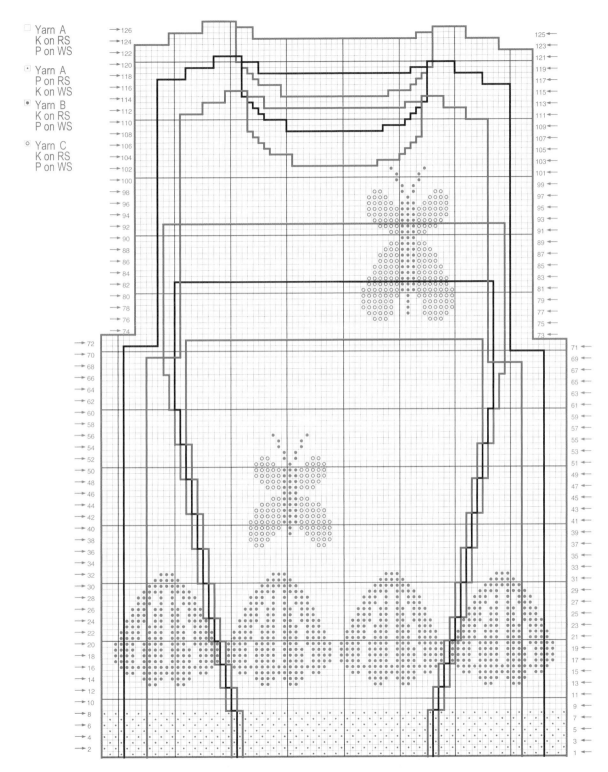

Sail Jacket

Age   1-2 years   2-3 years   3-4 years

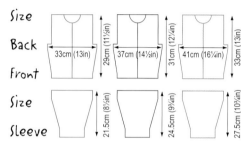

Size		
Back		
33cm (13in)	37cm (14½in)	41cm (16¼in)
29cm (11½in)	31cm (12¼in)	33cm (13in)
Front		
Size		
Sleeve		
21.5cm (8½in)	24.5cm (9¾in)	27.5cm (10¾in)

Yarn

Rowan Denim x 50g balls

A. Memphis	5	5	6
B. Ecru	2	2	3

Needles

1 pair 3 ¼ mm (US 3) needles for edging
1 pair 4 mm (US 6) needles for main body

Buttons 5

Tension

20 sts and 28 rows to 10cm measured over stocking stitch using 4 mm (US 6) needles before washing

Note The chart is for the jacket fronts and back only, work from written instructions for sleeves.

Back

Using 3 ¼ mm (US 3) needles and yarn A cast on 58,66,74 sts and work from chart A and written instructions as folls:
Chart row 1: Knit.
Chart row 2: Knit.

Cont in garter st until chart row 10 completed.
Change to 4 mm (US 6) needles, beg with a K row cont in st st and shape sides as folls:
Chart row 11: Inc into first st, knit to last st, inc into last st. (60,68,76 sts)
Cont from chart shaping sides by inc as indicated to 66,74,82 sts.
Work without further shaping until chart row 56,56,60 completed.
Shape armhole
Cast off 6 sts at the beg next 2 rows. (54,62,70 sts)
Now joining in and breaking off colours for stripe pattern as indicated on chart B work in st st until chart row 40,44,48 completed.
Shape shoulders and back neck
Cast off 5,6,7 sts at the beg next 2 rows.
Chart row 43,47,51: Cast off 5,6,7 sts, patt until 7,8,9 sts on RH needle, turn and leave rem sts on a holder.
Chart row 44,48,52: Cast off 3 sts, patt to end.
Cast off rem 4,5,6 sts.
Rejoin yarn to rem sts, cast off centre 20,22,24 sts, patt to end. (12,14,16 sts)
Chart row 44,48,52: Cast off 5,6,7 sts, patt to end. (7,8,9 sts)
Chart row 45,49,53: Cast off 3 sts, patt to end.
Cast off rem 4,5,6 sts.

Left Front

Using 3 ¼ mm (US 3) needles and yarn A, cast on 29,33,37 sts and work from chart A and written instructions as folls:
Chart row 1: Knit.
Chart row 2: Knit.
Cont in garter st until chart row 10 completed.
Change to 4 mm (US 6) needles, beg with a K row cont in st st and shape sides as folls:
Chart row 11: Inc into first st, knit to end. (30,34,38 sts)
Cont from chart shaping side by inc as indicated to 33,37,41 sts.
Work without further shaping until chart row 56,56,60 completed.
Shape armhole
Cast off 6 sts at the beg next row. (27,31,35 sts)
Work 1 row.
Now joining in and breaking off colours for stripe pattern as indicated on chart B work in st st until chart row 31,35,39 completed.
Shape front neck
Chart row 32,36,40: Cast off 5,6,7 sts, patt to end. (22,25,28 sts)
Work 1 row.

Chart row 34,38,42: Cast off 4 sts, patt to end.
Dec 1 st at neck edge on next 4 rows. (14,17,20 sts)
Work until chart row 40,44,48 completed.
Shape shoulder
Cast off 5,6,7 sts at the beg of next and foll alt row.
Work 1 row.
Cast off rem 4,5,6 sts.

Right Front

Using 3 ¼ mm (US 3) needles and yarn A cast on 29,33,37 sts and work from chart A and written instructions as folls:
Chart row 1: Knit.
Chart row 2: Knit.
Cont in garter st until chart row 10 completed.
Change to 4 mm (US 6) needles and work in st st from chart. Complete to match left front, foll chart for right front and reversing shaping.

Sleeves (both alike)

Note Sleeves are worked in a stripe sequence as foll
10 rows yarn A
10 rows yarn B
These 20 rows make up the stripe pattern.
Using 3 ¼ mm (US 3) needles and yarn A, cast on 34,36,38 sts and work from written instructions as fol
Chart row 1: Knit.
Chart row 2: Knit.
Cont in garter st until 10 rows in all completed.
Change to 4 mm (US 6) needles and yarn B.
Chart row 11: Inc into first st, knit to last st, inc into last st. (36,38,40 sts)
Chart row 12: Purl.
Work 4 rows in st st.
Keeping stripe sequence correct inc at each end of next row and every foll 6th row to 52,56,60 sts.
Work without further shaping until 72,82,92 rows in all completed. Cast off.

Buttonband

With RS of left front facing and using 3 ¼ mm (US 3) needles and yarn A pick up and knit 53,57,61 sts from start of neck shaping to cast on edge.
Row 1(WS): Knit.
Work 7 more rows in garter st.
Cast off knitwise (on WS).

Buttonhole band

With RS of right front facing and using 3 ¼ mm (US 3) needles pick up and knit 53,57,61 sts from cast on edge to start of neck shaping to cast on edge.
Row 1(WS): Knit.

ork 2 more rows in garter st.
ttonhole row (RS): K2, (yo, K2tog, K12,13,14)
imes, yo, K2tog, K1.
ork 4 more rows in garter st.
st off knitwise (on WS).

llar
ing 3 ¼ mm (US 3) needles cast on 70,74,78 sts.
ork 27,29,31 rows in garter st, ending with a RS
w. Cast off knitwise.

w in all ends and wash pieces as described on
ge 27.
n both shoulder seams using backstitch.
w cast on edge of collar in place, starting and
ding half way across front bands.
mplete as shown in making up instructions,
ge 48.
w on buttons to correspond with buttonholes.

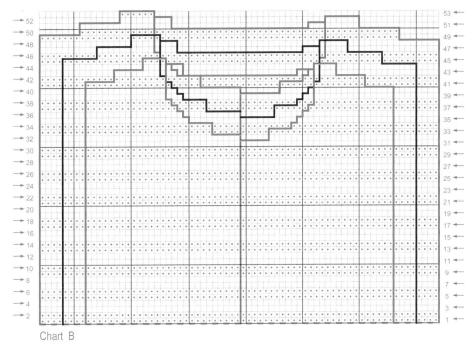

Chart B

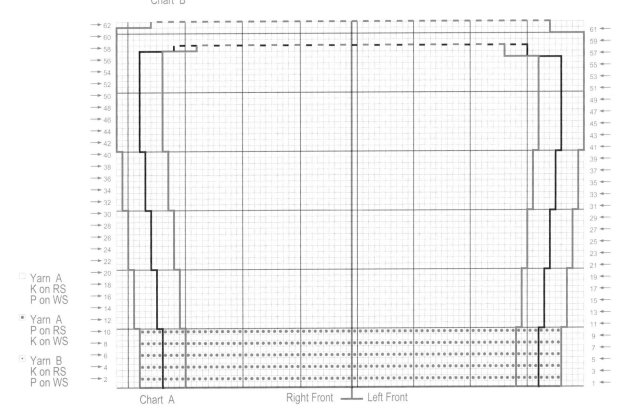

☐ Yarn A
  K on RS
  P on WS

⊙ Yarn A
  P on RS
  K on WS

⊡ Yarn B
  K on RS
  P on WS

Chart A

Right Front ⊥ Left Front

Knitting Techniques
A simple guide to making up and finishing

Putting your garment together

After spending many hours knitting it is essential that you complete your garment correctly. Following the written instructions and illustrations, we show you how easy it is to achieve a beautifully finished garment which will withstand the most boisterous child !

Pressing

With the wrong side of the fabric facing, pin out each knitted garment piece onto an ironing board using the measurements given in the size diagram. As each yarn is different, refer to the ball band and press pieces according to instructions given. Pressing the knitted fabric will help the pieces maintain their shape and give a smooth finish.

Sewing in ends

Once you have pressed your finished pieces, sew in all loose ends. Thread a darning needle with yarn, weave needle along approx 5 sts on wrong side of fabric; pull thread through. Weave needle in opposite direction approx 5 sts; pull thread through, cut end of yarn.

Making Up

If you are making a sweater join the right shoulder seam as instructed in the pattern, now work the neck edging. Join left shoulder seam and neck edging. If you are making a cardigan, join both shoulder seams as in the pattern and work edgings as instructed. Sew on buttons to correspond with buttonholes. Insert square set in sleeves as follows: Sew cast off edge of sleeve top into armhole. Making a neat right angle, sew in the straight sides at top of sleeve to cast off stitches at armhole. Join side and sleeve seams using either mattress stitch or back stitch. It is important to press each of the seams as you make the garment up.

Casting Off shoulder Seams together

This method secures the front and back shoulder stitches together, it also creates a small ridged seam. It is important that the cast off edge should be elastic like the rest of the fabric; if you find that your cast off is too tight, try using a larger needle. You can cast off with the seam on the right side (as illustrated) or wrong side of garment.

1. Place wrong sides of fabric together. Hold both needles with the stitches on in LH, insert RH needle into first stitch on both LH needles.

2. Draw the RH needle through both stitches.

3. Making one stitch on RH needle.

4. Knit the next stitch from both LH needles, two stitches on RH needle.

5. Using the point of one needle in LH, insert into first stitch on RH needle. Take the first stitch over the second stitch.

6. Repeat from 4 until one stitch left on right hand needle. Cut yarn and draw cut end through stitch to secure.

Picking Up Stitches

Once you have finished all the garment pieces, pressed them and sewn in all ends, you need to complete the garment by adding a neckband, front bands, or armhole edgings. This is done by picking up stitches along the edge of the knitted piece. The number of stitches to pick up is given in the pattern; these are made using a new yarn. When you pick up horizontally along a row of knitting it is important that you pick up through a whole stitch. When picking up stitches along a row edge, pick up one stitch in from the edge, this gives a neat professional finish.

1. Holding work in LH, with RS of fabric facing, insert RH needle into a whole stitch below the cast off edge, wrap new yarn around needle.

2. Draw the RH needle through fabric, making a loop with new yarn on right hand needle.

3. Repeat this action into the next stitch following the pattern instructions until all stitches have been picked up.

4. Work edging as instructed.

Mattress Stitch

This method of sewing up is worked on the right side of the fabric and is ideal for matching stripes. Mattress stitch should be worked one stitch in from edge to give the best finish. With RS of work facing, lay the two pieces to be joined edge to edge. Insert needle from WS between edge st and second st. Take yarn to opposite piece, insert needle from front, pass the needle under two rows, bring it back through to the front.

1. Work mattress stitch foundation as above.

2. Return yarn to opposite side working under two rows at a time, repeat.

3. At regular intervals gently pull stitches together.

4. The finished seam is very neat and almost impossible to see.

Back stitch

This method of sewing up is ideal for shoulder and armhole seams as it does not allow the fabric to stretch out of shape. Pin the pieces with right sides together. Insert needle into fabric at end, one stitch or row from edge, take the needle round the two edges securing them. Insert needle into fabric just behind where last stitch came out and make a short stitch. Re-insert needle where previous stitch started, bring up needle to make a longer stitch. Re-insert needle where last stitch ended. Repeat to end taking care to match any pattern.

Sewing in a Zip

With right side facing, neatly match row ends and slip stitch fronts of garment together. Pin zip into place, with right side of zip to wrong side of garment, matching centre front of garment to centre of zip. Neatly backstitch into place using a matching coloured thread. Undo slip stitches. Zip inserted.

Rowan Overseas Distributors

AUSTRALIA : Australian Country Spinners, 314 Albert Street, Brunswick, Victoria 3056. Tel : (03) 9380 3888

BELGIUM : Pavan, Meerlaanstraat 73, B9860 Balegem (Oosterzele). Tel : (32) 9 221 8594
Email : pavan@pandora.be

CANADA : Diamond Yarn, 9697 St Laurent, Montreal, Quebec, H3L 2N1. Tel :(514) 388 6188
Diamond Yarn (Toronto), 155 Martin Ross, Unit 3, Toronto, Ontario, M3J 2L9. Tel :(416) 736 6111
Email : diamond@diamondyarn.com URL : http://www.diamondyarn.com

DENMARK : Please contact Rowan for stockist details.

FRANCE : Elle Tricot, 8 Rue du Coq, 67000 Strasbourg. Tel : (33) 3 88 23 03 13.
Email : elletricot@agat.net

GERMANY : Wolle & Design, Wolfshovener Strasse 76, 52428 Julich-Stetternich. Tel : (49) 2461 54735.
Email : Info@wolleunddesign.de URL : http://www.wolleunddesign.de

HOLLAND : de Afstap, Oude Leliestraat 12, 1015 AW Amsterdam. Tel : (31) 20 6231445.

HONG KONG : East Unity Co Ltd, Unit B2, 7/F, Block B, Kailey Industrial Centre, 12 Fung Yip Street, Chai Wan.
Tel : (852) 2869 7110. Fax : (852) 2537 6952
Email : eastuni@netvigator.com

ICELAND : Storkurinn, Laugavegi 59,101 Reykjavik. Tel : (354) 551 8258 Fax : (354) 562 8252
Email : malin@mmedia.is

JAPAN : Puppy Co Ltd, TOC Building, 7-22-17 Nishigotanda, Shinagawa-ku, Tokyo. Tel : (81) 3 3494 2435.
Email : info@rowan-jaeger.com

KOREA : De Win Co Ltd, Chongam Bldg, 101, 34-7 Samsung-dong, Seoul.
Tel : (82) 2511 1087. E mail : dewin@dewin.co.kr. URL : http://www.dewin.co.kr

NEW ZEALAND : Please contact Rowan for stockist details.

NORWAY : Paa Pinne, Tennisvn 3D, 0777 Oslo. Tel : (47) 909 62 818.
Email : design@paapinne.no URL : http://www.paapinne.no

SWEDEN : Wincent, Norrtullsgaten 65, 113 45 Stockholm. Tel : (46) 8 33 70 60 Fax : (46) 8 33 70 68.
Email : wincent@chello.se URL : http://www.wincent.nv

TAIWAN : Green Leave, No 181, Sec 4, Chung Ching N. Road, Taipei, Taiwan R.O.C. Tel : (886) 2 8221 2925.
Chien He Wool Knitting Co, 10 -1 313 Lane, Sec 3, Cmung-Ching North Road, Taipei, Taiwan. Tel : (886) 2 2596 0269

U.S.A : Rowan USA, 4 Townsend West, Suite 8, Nashua, New Hampshire 03063. Tel : (1 603) 886 5041 / 5043.
Email : rowan@westminsterfibers.com

UNITED KINGDOM : Green Lane Mill, Holmfirth,West Yorkshire, HD9 2DX. Tel : (44) (0) 1484 681881.
Email : missbea@knitrowan.com URL : http://www.knitrowan.com